THE NEW BIZARRO AUTHOR SERIES

PRESENTS

I0630138

BENJAMIN

Pedro Proença

Eraserhead Press
Portland, OR

ERASERHEAD PRESS
P.O. BOX 10065
PORTLAND, OR 97296

WWW.ERASERHEADPRESS.COM

ISBN: 1-62105-200-1

Printed in the USA.

There's this great phenomenon in Bizarro that has contributed to the genre's success in fascinating ways. Some Bizarro fans become microcelebs in their own right. If you are a Bizarro fan, you are as likely to have heard of Raye Roeske or Erika Instead as you are of…well, me. If you are in Bizarro fan circles, you are excited to hold this motherfucker in your hand. And you should be. Pedro is a celebrity Bizarro superfan, the kind of fan that puts the "Leave Britney Alone!" dude to shame.

He is a giant Brazilian bass prodigy with infectious cheer, a love of shirtlessness and a Blue/Red counterburn deck that will eat your fucking heart. He is also a hell of a writer. Imaginative, hardworking and brave, he has bulldozed through the boundaries of language and culture to bring you a beautiful and transgressive dream. Benjamin is the story of a yellow balloon seeking meaning and what meaning means to us.

This book is cool. I say this about all these books and I have yet to lie to you fine people.

— Garrett Cook, Editor

To Sarah,
who always stood by me.

And to my family,
that made me the man I am today

Chapter One
Enter the Ballon

"You're awfully quiet, dear, what's on your mind?"

Benjamin looks out the bookstore's window, careful not to move not even an inch, as the bookseller talks to him. His hat is balancing dangerously on his head, and the last thing he wants is to draw her attention more than necessary.

"Please, Benji, talk to me."

He wasn't always called Benjamin. In fact, he wasn't called anything. He simply existed.

Benjamin is a balloon. A yellow balloon, with a smiley face drawn on with a Sharpie. He has a string dangling from his bottom. Attached to the string, there is the Boy. He's sitting on the arm of the couch, frozen in position, always keeping Benjamin steady. He has no head.

The name Benjamin is already familiar in the balloon's mind.

This is in spite of the fact that he has no mind. Not a physical one at least. Inside of him, there's only air.

The bookseller – Karen – approaches Benjamin, ignoring the Boy completely. She caresses the Benjamin's back, causing him to drop his hat.

"Oopsy daisy, let me get that for you, honey," she says, though she makes no effort to pick it up.

Karen's husband died when they were newlyweds. She's fifty five going on eighty and she never got over his death, burying herself in books and several cats throughout the years.

His name was Benjamin.

"Benjamin, if you don't talk to me right now, you'll get no dinner!"

As she is talking, the Boy takes Benjamin's hat from the floor and placed it on the balloon.

"Thank you, son," Benjamin says. The Boy has no ears (because of the no head thing) and the balloon has no actual mouth, but somehow they are able to comunicate . The Boyis the only living being with whom Benjamin can estabilsh some kind of comunication. And the headless child can't answer back.

Karen stands beside Benjamin, her arms crossed. Fred, her big brown cat, is sleeping on a pillow by the store's counter. She completely ignores the Boy picking up the hat. Her right foot taps on the floor impatiently. She demands an answer from her husband, the husband that was dead for thirty years and whom she found floating through the mall, abducted, and took home .

All Benjamin can do is to float in place, held on by the Boy and the string, staring at the empty mall, longing for freedom. And watching as Karen storms out of the room dodging the few bookcases spread though the tiny store, and heads to her makeshift bedroom on the back of the bookstore, listening to her muffled cries as she throws herself on the bed.

***

Green men walk through the mall at night. Benjamin watches them from his spot behind the window. They are just walking about, like they're window shopping. One of them stops in front of an electronics store, and signals another one to come have a look. He waves excitedly, rushing his friend, like the most interesting thing in the world is on display right before their eyes.

They have short strands of hair on their head, and are completely naked.

Besides being green, they are completely flat. No nipples, no penises. And Benjamin notices they have six fingers on each hand. He sees it when the excited one begins stroking the window of the store they are staring at.

The Boy gets up and walks around the bookstore. He stops by Fred, still sleeping on his corner, and pets him lightly.

Benjamin was never actually trapped in the bookstore. He simply pities Karen.

He instructs the Boy to take him to the backroom. As the door creaks open, Karen wakes up.

"Benjamins," she says, wiping her eyes. The balloon notices the tear- stained pillow and the bags under her eyes.

"I need you to see this, Karen," Benjamin says in his mind. Again he has lost his hat, there is only floating yellow latex in front of the tired bookseller. And still, all she sees is her husband.

"I knew you'd come back. Benji, I've missed you so much!" She's crying now, and hugging Benjamin tight. He's not worried, he knows he's not going to pop. But still feels sad, for she hasn't gotten the message.

"Karen, you need to come right now!" he says again, screaming though the void that is his mind. He imagines the drawn up face on his body frowning and twisting, expressing anger, but all it does is to remain smiling, as if nothing were wrong.

"I love you, baby," she says, sobbing, her body relaxing once more as she hugs Benjamin. The Boy has to pick her up before she falls on the floor, still hugging the balloon, and place her back in the bed.

"I love you too, Karen. I bet he'd say that. Let's go, Boy,

9

we need to do something."

The Boy slowly stumbles out the bedroom door dragging Benjamin by his string. They stop by the bookstore window.

Two of the green men continue to watch the electronics store's window. There are five of them in Benjamin's line of sight. The other three were just standing around, checking their inexistent fingernails for dirt ou picking their inexistent teeth with toothpicks. Trying as hard as they could to act casual.

"It's happening again," the ballooon thought.

Benjamin has heard rumors (or at least he has the memory of hearing it; he isn't sure of anything since before his incarceration at the bookstore) of troubles. A disease, corrupting the very soul of the mall he lived on. He suspects the green men have something to do with it.

A loud crash. Then several more.

Benjamin turns back and sees the Boy has knocked over the counter trying to pet Fred. The cat has jumped from his spot and landed on one of the small bookcases, knocking it over.

Several loud crashes followed as the cases dominoed around the room.

And at the same time, Karen flicks her bedroom light as the green men converge on the bookstore's window.

"Oh no, son," Benjamin transmits to the Boy. He's not really mad, he can't be really. He just knows what's going to happen next.

Karen stumbles out of the room, wiping her eyes. She first sees the toppled cases; then her cat panting, his hair standing up; and finally, a naked green man pulling his fist back, preparing to break her window.

She screams as the glass shatters, and the strange men swarm her store.

The Boy is standing in the same place since scaring the cat. He moves no muscle, as if was trying to blend in the enviroment.

Benjamin watch as the green men grab a screaming Karen and pull her out of the store. Her skin is bruised by the broken glass.

One green man stops in front of Benjamin. His skin is smooth and oily, like a salamander's.

"Hello, friend," the green man says. He *hisses.* "Haven't seen you in a while." He caresses Benjamin's yellow latex with his six fingered hand.

"Son," Benjamin says in his mind. A book flies by fast, hitting the green man square in the face.

"AHHHH!" the green man screams.

"Let's go," Benjamin says. The Boy moves in long strides, snatches the string away from the green man and jumps through the broken window, effortlessly. No bruised skin.

The Boy rushes past the other four green men who are holding Karen andmoving her slowly through the mall. Although they must have heard their companion's scream, they make no effort to help him.

"Save Karen, son.," Benjamin says.

The Boy just keeps running.

"What are you doing?." Benjamin sounds confused. He *is* confused, especially by the fact the green man seemed to know him, and also because the Boy is not listening to his orders for the first time since he can remember.

"Boy, turn back, we need to save her."

The headless boy just keeps running towards the food court, the first strands of sunlight coming in through the mall's skylight.

"Please, son, what are you doing? Why aren't you

listening to me?"

Benjamin looks to the Boy's other hand, and sees Fred the cat being carried rather rudely, hissing and waving his paw around. He almost hits Benjamin.

"Oh, I see. You want to get your friend into safety. But we must go back, we must save the woman. Please, son, listen to me."

The Boy stops cold in his tracks. Benjamin notices they are in front of PET PLAYGROUND, Mr. Daniels' pet store.

Benjamin realizes what the Boy wants to do, and instead of stopping him, tells him to do it fast.

The Boy kicks the glass window, triggering the alarm.

"That's right, there's an alarm...why didn't it go off when the green men got into the bookstore?" Benjamin thinks, as the Boy jumps inside the pet store, puts Fred in a cat carrier, and closes the lid.

"Now, go."

The Boy runs back, never sweating or slowing down. He's an obese headless teenager, but shows incredible agility and stamina. The two of them reach the bookstore, but there's no sign of the green men.

"There!" Benjamin says loudly in the Boy's mind, planting the image of pair of green legs entering the woman's bathroom down the hall.

Benjamin urges the Boy to run faster, but as they enter the bathroom, they see the following:

The five green men are standing in front of the last stall from the door. The stall's door is open, and a purple-ish light emanates from where the toilet must be.

"Here it is, lad, take it all in," the same green man who acosted Benjamin says, as the other four toss Karen's unconscious body up and into the stall.

"No...," Benjamin thinks, just as a purple/black tentacle

emerges from the toilet and wraps around Karen's waist. It wraps and wraps, constricting the bookeeper's body, until a loud crack ensues.

The Boy moves as to attack the men, but Benjamin mentally holds him back.

"She's dead, son, there's nothing we can do."

Just then, the green man who was hit by the Boy turns to them, standing by the door.

"You defeated us once, fiend, but not again. We will rule this existence once more, and you won't be even a memory."

The five green men jump towards the tentacle at the same time. The very touch of the bizarre appendage on their body turns each of them in a pile of green goo. The tentacle proceeds to suck the remains with its suction cups, and retreats back into his toilet realm.

Chapter Two
Toilet Troubles

The Boy pets Fred as Benjamin looks around the food court.

There's people everywhere, doing all sort of things: Eating greasy fast food; passing by in a hurry, late for something, passing by camly, window shopping as they chat with a friend or a significant other, just sittig on one of the tables, groups of friends and loners alike.

"If only they knew," thinks Benjamin.

Fred purrs on the Boy's lap. He's been close to the big headless kid since his owner disappeared.

To put it lightly.

Benjamin watches the movers clearing out the bookstore. Books are placed in cardboard boxes and hauled out carelessly, shelves are dismantled and the counter is simply discarded, the wood rotten in several places.

"Look on my works, ye Patty, and despair!"

The man sits besides the Boy and Benjamin. He's about fifty, wearing a faded green zoot suit, and a red fedora. He's something out of a cartoon, thinks Benjamin. He reaches out towards the Boy, and if Benjamin could flinch, he would. The man just strokes Fred, whose hair stands up with the contact of that strange hand. Benjamin notices that the hand, although normal shaped, is scaly and grey.

"I like that name for you, Patty. Are you a girl? You look like one."

The man just pets the cat absently, his eyes fixated on the now almost empty bookstore.

"I had a cat named Patty once, she was my special friend.

14

Where I'd go, she went. We went through the good times and the bad times together. I miss her very much."

Benjamin can see the man is not paying attention to him or the Boy. He mentally signals his friend to drop Fred down and go.

The Boy does not move.

"Listen, let go of the cat. He'll be safe in the mall. Let's just get away from this creature."

Fred has calmed down now, and accepts more of the man's petting. Sometimes, the man's weird hand brushes against the Boy's, but he doesn't seem to notice. He can only see his "Patty."

"I've miss you so much, girl," the man says. There are tears streaming down his eyes now. He stops petting Fred and buries his face in his hands, sobbing.

"Now!" Benjamin says.

With a new display of his odd agility, the Boy gets up in one swift motion, Fred in one hand and Benjamin's string in the other, and starts to scurry away from the strange, crying man.

"I'm so glad I ate that whore you were with," the man says, still holding his face, the crying now gone.

Benjamin jolts a command so sudden, the Boy almost trips when he stops walking.

"You see, thing, I loved my Patty, and I know you're not her. You're not even a cat, are you? You're just some yellow, rubbery thing. You're pathetic!"

No one is paying attention to the altercation, Benjamin notices. He looks around, and realises everyone in the mall is frozen in place, completely paralyzed

"Who are you?" Benjamin thinks.

"I'm your worst nightmare, baby," the man says.

Benjamin suddenly sees himself, the man, the Boy,

everything frozen. He's a spectator watching a play within four walls, those walls being the mall's background relative to the main players' positions. He sees his smiling face, unchanging as time itself; the Boy, stading firmly, his lack of head (and thus, of face) masking whatever he may be feeling at the moment; Fred, the cat-who-is-not-Patty in the Boy's arms, sleeps quietly like any irrational being in the midst of something he can't understand; the man, his colorful visage appearing as a stark contrast to the whiteness and cleanliness of the shopping mall. He sees all of this from a floating position, a sensation of freedom he had never experienced before, even in his free floating balloon form.

And from this position, Benjamin watches as the background melts. The stores, the fast food places, the people walking or sitting, the tables, everything just melts away, like a bad painting too close to a fireplace. He feels light-headed as his environment drips away, revealing the truth: He's still in the women's bathroom.

Something snaps, and Benjamin is seeing the world through his own painted-on eyes again. It feels like that moment just after a movie projector turns on, and the film clicks into place.

There is a group of green men standing by a stall, staring at him. Benjamin is held by the Boy, and the balloon laments the fact he can't possibly tell what the Boy is thinking right now, if anything at all.

Everything seems clearer now. Benjamin somehow recalls the earlier scene, when he and the Boy were watching the movers empty Karen's bookstore. Looking back, it seemed fake to him.

"No, it didn't. Stop trying to rationalize this," he thinks to himself.

"Yes, balloon" A voice coming from the last stall.

The tentacle bursts through the toilet lid, blasting it to the ceiling. It flips and flops around, spraying the green men in sickly goo. They explode with contact, smearing the walls with their green, strange insides.

"What are you?" Benjamin asks.

"I am your father, Benjamin." He says the word Benjamin in an imitation of Karen's high, weepy voice.

Benjamin turns to the Boy.

"No, but I could be. I mean, I'm just a disgusting, reality bending toilet monster, but I could be your father. What the fuck do you know about yourself, balloon?" the man says.

"Run," Benjamin says, and the Boy obliges.

They run past the door, the Boy being careful as to not slip on any green man residue.

Laughter follows them out.

"You better run, boy! And don't let me caught you stealing my prized petunias again! HAHAHAHAHAHAHAHAHA"

The Boy runs as fast as he can, dragging Benjamin behind. The balloon feels light, lighter than usual, he can't collect his thoughts.

"What is happening?" he thinks.

"Run, piggy, run!" the man's voice come from behind.

They both keep running, Benjamin still feeling strange.

Soon, they reach the food court again.

"Sit down, son, he wouldn't show himself here." Somehow, the mall is open, and people are everywhere. They must have been in the women's bathroom for hours.

The Boy sits on an empty table. His breathing is troubled from all the running. Benjamin wishes he could

"Calm down, we're probably safe right now."

At this moment, they feel one of the chair's legs sinking, throwing the Boy off his balance.

"Not again," thinks Benjamin.

The whole food court floor begins to crumble. People panic, scrambling to get some balance as the literal floor beneath them is taken away.

Benjamin hears splatter as people begin to fall through the gaping floor, blood burst upwards with sickly noises. He and the Boy cling on, jumping from place to place, trying to escape the collapsing hall.

As they approach safety, the last piece breaks and they fall down...

...and land safely on their feet, in the woman's bathroom.

Benjamin and the Boy find themselves again before the green men and the cursed stall.

"This is fun!" says the voice from the toilet. "We should do this more often!" it says, as the tentacle shoots up again, turning the static green men into jelly.

The bathroom doors opens.

A janitor comes walking by, with a bucket and a mop. He hums a melody.

Benjamin, the Boy and the waving tentacle protruding from the toilet all stop. They watch silently as the janitor begins mopping up the floor, seemingly oblivious to their quarrel. He mops away the green men's goo, dunking his mop in the bucket from time to time. He takes his sweet time scrubbing to make sure that the floor is spotless.

He then goes to the last stall, where the tentacle is. He frowns, unfazed by the supernatural entity he's seeing.

"Well, this don't look right," he says, as he reaches for his back pocket and retrieves a plunger.

"Must have been that ol' fat Mr. Littlewood eating his own junk food again," says the janitor, waving his head in disapproval. Mr. Littlewood does in fact eat pretty poorly. He is the manager of Hardy's, a fast food restaurant that specializes in recipes with ramen noodles and chicken nuggets.

The janitor stabs away with the plunger, apparently mistaking a monster who can bend reality at will for a big turd left by the manager of a terrible fast food place.

"No, wait, wait a minute," says the tentacle, but the janitor does not hear him. He just keeps on humming as he plunges away.

Benjamin and the Boy hear the toilet monster's screams as it descends back down the toilet. And, seconds later, a flushing noise, as the janitor walks out after proudly doing his job.

The janitor grabs his mop and bucket and inspect the walls for more stains or general filth..

"You shouldn't mess around with that thing," says the janitor, looking right at Benjamin.

"I'm not going to bother asking if you can see me or the Boy, because you clearly do," says the balloon. "I'm just going to thank you for helping us."

"I didn't do anything. That beast shapes reality as he pleases, and the thought of an old man with a plunger who can't see him for what he really is, is enough to send him back down temporarily. It's too absurd, even for him. But, we should talk about getting rid of him for good, don't you agree?"

Benjamin does. He knows so little about himself, about the Boy. His whole existence seem to have began at Karen's bookstore, with no background or explanation given.

"Do you want to go somewhere to talk?" says Benjamin.

"Oh no, not now. We need to take some precautions. There are a few of us who know what's really going on in this place, and we have a weekly meeting on a secret location."

Benjamin notices the man seems a lot younger when he speaks. When the janitor first entered the bathroom, Benjamin would have guessed he was sixty five, seventy.

But now, hearing the man speak, Benjamin gave him fifty, at max.

"When can we talk, then?"Benjamin asks. We is impatient, he needs answers.

"I'll find you. Tonight, around seven thirty-ish. Just stay out of trouble, and avoid the Nexus. I know you don't know what that is, but that's ok, just hearing about something to avoid will make you more careful. I could have said anything really, like 'avoid the Noid', and you'd be on your toes...I mean, string. Just be ready for a surprise meeting later tonight," the janitor says, with a big smile on his face.

Benjamin thinks it over. He needs to talk with the boy

"Wait a minute," Benjamin says. "How can it be a surprise meeting, if I already know about it?"

But the janitor is already humming his way out of the bathroom, and from behind, Benjamin again saw him as a decrepit old man. Only now he knew better.

"Let's go, son," Benjamin says. "For some reason, I'm dying for some ice cream right now."

Chapter Three
Books and Ice Cream

Benjamin has never had ice cream before, nor can he actually do so.. He's a balloon. So he and the Boy just sit on an empty table at the food court and look at the people. Benjamin notices people looking at the two of them, which is something that never happened before. They were never seen, just blending with the environment. But now, people nudge each other, pointing and whispering, looking at the strange headless boy holding up a balloon.

"Is it okay if I sit here?" says a girl approaching their table.

Benjamin looks at her: About sixteen, black dress, bleached blond hair, almost white. Blue eyes. No nose.

"Please, be our guest," says Benjamin.

The girl sits, not making eye contact with neither Benjamin (his painted on eyes are weird to look at for prolonged periods of time) nor the Boy (again, headless). She has a messenger bag across her chest, from which she produces a book. Benjamin reads the title on the cover: *When The Postman Killed My Dog*, by Benjamin Jensen. He's filled with a sudden unease after reading the book's title, the same feeling he had when reality melted and he found himself standing on the women's bathroom once again. He looks around, trying to spot any signs of melting, but there is none. He grounds himself, looking at the Boy, the people, listening to the sounds of chatter, of walking. He calms himself down.

"Interesting title," says Benjamin.

"Yep," the noseless girl says. She's smilling at Benjamin,

21

a shy smile, like she's trying to hide it.

Benjamin is not used to small talk. He feels unconfortable around the girl, but also mildly pleased. He's beginning to like being seen.

"What it is about?"

The Boy's leg is now shaking. He's stomping the floor lightly. Benjamin thinks he's nervous. He too is not accustumed to social interaction.

"You should know, you wrote it," says the girl.

That hits him like a tiny sharp needle. Benjamin immediately thinks of something the janitor had said.

"Do you know about the Nexus?" he asks the girl.

"Of course, I'm reading your book, you talk about it in the first chapter. See?"

She opens the book to page 12 and shows it to Benjamin, who instantly issues a mental command to the Boy to grab him and walk away.

"Hey, where are you going? I'd really love your autograph, I was just too shy to ask!" the noseless girl says.

"Just keep on going, son, just keep on going," Benjamin says.

They stop by the ice cream stand and sit on one of those standing tables you usually find by a quick stop establishment, with an umbrella running through the middle, even though it's an indoors ice cream stand in a mall.

Benjamin looks back and sees the girl hasn't followed them, but she isn't sitting at their table anymore. He sees no sign of her.

"What can I get you, mister?" says the ice cream man, a dwarf with a big head. No, really, a hugely oversized, cartoonesque, giant head. His eyes are silver, like embedded coins, and he has a Dick Dastardly mustache.

"I love Wacky Races, used to watch with my dad all the

time," the man says, reading Benjamin's mind.

Benjamin is somehow unfazed by that.

"Sorry, I seem to have dozed off there. Hummm, I never really had ice cream before. As you can see, I'm-"

"A balloon, yes, I can see that. But I have a special line of ice cream that can be absorbed through latex!" the man says, rubbing his tiny hands together in a rather villainous sort of way.

That cheers Benjamin, but then immediately saddens him.

"I'd love one of those, but I don't have any money," he says.

"No problem, amigo! I can't let you, a poor balloon who never even known the taste of ice cream leave here empty stringed. Here you go, a free balloon-friendly Passion Fruit Delight!"

The Boy picks up the cone produced by the ice cream man. Benjamin asks him to hold up so he can inspect it. He can't smell it, but he knows from its creamy texture and bright color that it must be a heavenly treat.

"So, what do I do? I just have him smear it all over my face?

The ice cream man leans forward, smiling creeply.

"No no, that's not necessary, my friend. You see, a balloon is much like a black hole. Nothing can escape from your insides, not even light. Everything is sucked by your gravitational pull. But, as recent findings show, the information sucked by a balloon is not stored in its gas-filled interior, but instead, on its event horizon, that area close enough of the latex surface where you're not touching the balloon, but can feel some static electricity if you rub it on a piece of wool. So, all you have to do to enjoy my delicious present is to have your beautiful, almost complete

Boy take the ice cream really close to your exterior, and just hold it there for a few seconds. The ice cream will be sucked by the event horizon, creating a hologram of itself that will be expelled out by Hawking radiation, containing all the information of the original ice cream, in the form of disgusting, semi digested bile."

"I like the sound of that," says Benjamin, mentally licking his non-existent lips.

"So, eat away, my friend!"

Benjamin commands the boy to do as instructed. The Boy does not move.

"Come on, son, I'm dying here. Let me have some of that sweet release."

The Boy lets go of Benjamin, causing the balloon to float aimlessly, and runs away, tossing the ice cream on the floor as he goes.

"What the hell...," Benjamin says.

The Dick Dastardly ice cream man becomes enraged. His enourmous face swells even more, turning bright red, his legal tender eyes becoming like cannonballs.

"Come back here, you cocksucker! I need the Nexus, feed the balloon!" he yells.

At the mention of the elusive Nexus, Benjamin feels like he is waking from a dream.

"What did you say?" he asks the ice cream man.

"I need you! I need you to get the Nexus! Please, eat the ice cream, I need your digestive juices! Please, here, have some more, have the whole stand, I can give it to you!"

Benjamin feels vulnerable. Without the Boy, he has no means of transportation, no way to defend himself from the mad man.

"Here, have some Chocolate Daydream. Better yet, some Condensed Milk Paradise, a favorite on cold, rainy days. Or some more Passion Fruit Delight, I don't care, just suck this shit inside you and give me your juices!"

The blazing man grabs a yellow creamy cone and jumps the stand counter.

"I want you, Nexus! I'll be there shortly!" he screams, approaching Benjamin. The balloon is filled with dread. Suddenly he doesn't want the creamy, sweet goodness of the Passion Fruit Delight. He feels disconnected somehow. He's been feeling this way since people have started talking to him.

"Boy, help me!" Benjamin screams in his mind. He can't see the Boy anywhere. He feels alone as he never felt before.

The ice cream man has madness on his face. His head is now completely swollen and red, his mustache seems to move in unnatural ways.

"I've got you now, Nexus!" he says as he charges Benjamin, ice cream cone in hand.

A large, gray cilinder descends upon the ice cream man from above, sending him flying across the room just as he was about to reach Benjamin.

The balloon looks up, and surely enough, the Boy is riding an elephant and saving him.

"Thank you, my son."

Benjamin thinks he's heard a sound in his head.

"Could it be...?"

From behind the elephant the Boy is riding comes another one, this one ridden by the janitor.

"Well, hello Benjamin. I see you're having some troubles with one of our fine employees."

The balloon stays in place, unsure of what to say to the janitor. He promised he would stay away from the Nexus, but the Nexus found him again and again.

"Hello to you, sir, and thank you for rescuing me. May I ask, where did you found these fine looking animals?"

"In our movie theater, of course, they are our screen."

Benjamin wasn't fully sure he understood that, but talking made him dizzy. He still needed to get used to communicating with people other than the Boy.

That reminded him of something.

"Say, do you happen to know a girl without a nose? Teenager, blonde, black dress? Carrying a messenger bag?"

The janitor scratches his chin with one hand while petting the elephant with the other.

"You know, that's a mighty fine good question, Mr. Balloon. One I'm sure we could find an asnwer to in our secret meeting tonight."

"You mean the secret meeting I'm somehow supposed to be prepared for?"

The janitor grins, and Benjamin somehow feels better.

"Why, yes, that's the one. As our special guest, you don't even need to enter our food buying spreadsheet. Tonight, snacks and drinks are on the house!"

The janitor lets out a hearty laugh at this, as if the thought of a balloon eating some chips and dip is the funniest thing in the world.

Benjamin can't help be contaminated by the janitor's laugh, even as he notices the ice cream man disappearing down a hall, looking back with an angered expression suggesting revenge.

"So, Mr. Balloon, tell your obedient kid to take you to the Wires'R'Us tonight at seven. You know that place, right?"

Benjamin did. It was the electronics store that mesmerized the green men who took Karen away.

"We'll be there," he says, signalling the Boy to come pick him up.

He doesn't feel like ice cream any more and doubts he ever would again.

26

Chapter Four
The Secret Meeting

Looking at Karen's boarded up store, Benjamin thinks of books.

One particular book, really.

When The Postman Killed My Dog.

The noseless girl said he had written a book. She even gave him a last name – Jensen.

He has no memory of ever writing a book. The implications if he did were endless.

Was he, at some point in time, a human? At least he needed hands to write the book. Although, he could have dictated the text to someone. But before the janitor, the only person who could understand him was the Boy.

Benjamin looks at the headless Boy.

"Son, are you my amanuensis?" he asks, sort of proud of himself for using the word amanuensis in a sentence.

The Boy says nothing. He just pets Fred, who's been living in the mall and sometimes finds the Boy for some petting and cuddling.

"No, of course not," the balloon thinks.

He wonders if Karen's booksore carries his book.

His book. The thought is strange to him.

"She must have carried it at some point. To her, I was her husband. She must have had many copies of his – of *my* – book."

With a mental command, the Boy gently places a sleeping Fred in the artificial flower bed in the center of the hallway and carries Benjamin closer to the bookstore.

"The boxes of books are stil there, son. Could you break through some of these boards? I shouldn't have pushed the noseless girl away. I was told to avoid the Nexus, avoid it at any cost, but I need to know. I need to see it for myself."

The Boy grabs the closest board and begins forcing it out.

"Hey kid, whatcha doin'?"

A large fat man comes walking by. He's wearing a security guard uniform, but surely no establishment could hire such a morbidly obese man for security.

The man wobbles towards the Boy, and stops short, clutching his chest.

"Dammit, the ticker is goin' at it again." His accent is a mixture of Italian-American and Brazilian. So, lot's of *ayyyy*s and hissing *S*s.

He stumbles forward, his face contorted in pain.

"Grab him, son!" Benjamin says.

The Boy just stands still while the man withers in pain on the ground.

Not for the first time, Benjamin feels completely powerless. The Boy was ignoring his commands again, and it was becoming more often. He depends on the chubby headless Boy to be his physical body.

"Don't let him die!" Benjamin says. He *screams.*

The Boy jumps up, high. Benjamin admires him, as he moves through the air almost as if in slow motion. He dances in the sky, an impossibly fat body filled with grace and magnificence.

He lands on the obese security guard knee first, right on the chest.

The man lets out a howl of pain and relief. He gasps for air as the Boy stumbles up, pulling on his butt crack revealing jeans.

"Yep, 'twas the ticker alrite," says the man, reaching his hand up as if asking for help to get to his feet, and getting up by himself when none comes.

He opens his shirt, revealing an opening right on the left side of his chest. Inside, there is a small canary in a silver cage, fitted where the man's heart should be. The canary looks like it is singing, but no sound is coming from its beek. The cage was held together in two points, on top and on bottom, by steel clamps. The Boy's knee dislodges the cage back into place, where it ias spinning, the canary always in the same position, as if a mechanical music box with no sound.

"The old fella likessss to play tricks on me, the bugger. I love him to death, but he can be a real motherfucker."

"I'm glad you're alright," says Benjamin.

"Ohh, it's nothin', it happens all the time. Your little freak here helped me quite nicely, that's why I'm not takin' him in for tryin' to rob the old lady's bookstore."

Benjamin takes offense to this.

"First of all, sir, my Boy is no freak. Second, he wasn't trying to rob anything; he was just helping me find a book I may or may not have written, that maybe lies on one of those boxes."

The security guard scratches his balding head, finds what looks like a piece of food, nibbles on it, makes a face, and feeds the rest of it to the canary, who interrupts its mimic singing to munch on the find.

"So, you wrote a book, b'loony?." It sounds almost like *bologna.*

"Well, I don't really remember, no. I may have."

The man keeps on scratching and feeding. He squint his eys.

"So...that book you may or may not have written is in

29

there, in Miss Karen's shop?"

Benjamin feels glad for his permanent smile, because he's realizing the situation.

"I don't know. I think so. She did think I was her husband, so it's logical she kept a copy of a book I may have written."

Silence from the security guard. The absurdity is too much, even for a man with a bird's cage instead of a heart.

"Okay, that's it, I'm out of here," says a booming, James Earl Jones-like voice.

It's the canary.

"Too much freaky shit is going down for my taste, I can't handle it. I'm hauling ass, you dig?"

It says this while collecting a really small suitcase and a really small fedora. It opens its cage and jumps, not so much flying as levitating, sending off with a "See you, suckers!"

"Oh sssshit," says the obese guard, as he collapses on the ground, sweating profusely and panting, out of breath.

Benjamin sends a mental command to the Boy, but a hand catches the canary in mid air.

"Oh, hi, little fellow," says the janitor.

"You're not supposed to kill Mr. Vinogradov over here. He's your friend, remember?"

The janitor steps up to the dying man, and sticks the canary in his chest cage, locking it with a key he produces from his pocket.

"You shouldn't leave this laying around, Vinogradov," says the janitor as he helps the guard up.

"Thanks, sir. Yeah, the wee bastard can't handle one tiny slice of absurdity before it's already trying to flee," says the fat security guard, downplaying the fact he was just as perturbed by the balloon's story as his bird heart.

The janitor smiles, as always.

"He's just not connected with the fabric of reality like us

people are. While to us absurdity is the cake that feeds, to him it's the poison that kills. Now move along, I hear someone threw up on a cashier at Hardy's and it's now taking selfies with her, not letting her wash up."

"Sonofabitch!" screams the guard, as he runs towards the food court. He lasts for about ten seconds before collapsing on the floor. The janitor and Benjamin watch the canary flying away from the guard's still body before turning to each other.

"No matter where I find you, there's trouble around, Mr. Balloon," says the janitor.

Benjamin doesn't answer.

"Are you ready for our meeting?"

"Yes, looking forward to it," says Benjamin.

"Good, let's go, it's time."

"I thought it was tonight, it still early."

The janitor's smile opens up even more.

"It is night, Benjamin, look around."

Benjamin does, and sees the mall is covered in twilight. The stores are closed, the doors bolted shut. A tree sprouted from the body of the guard and grew up to the roof. Its fruits are large, red spheres. From afar, Benjamin thinks he sees patches of thin hair on them.

"Yes, I guess you're right, Mr. Janitor. Lead us there," says the balloon.

The janitor points them the way to the Wires'R'Us

"I saw one of the green men staring at something in this window, which is now empty," says Benjamin as they walk through the store's front door, that was open for some reason.

The janitor does not acknowledge.

"In here, please, Benjamin. You too, son."

They walk through the large store, heading towards the back room. In there, the janitor pulls a lever on one of the walls, revealing a secret trapdoor. They walk down the spiral staircase into what's clearly meant to be an intimidating secret room.

It's got balconies on its four walls, and on each one there is a cloaked figure standing. On the center, there is a podium, where the janitor positions himself in. He nods to a chair right in front of himself, where the Boy sits, holding Benjamin by the string.

"So, we are all gathered here tonight to talk to our new friend, Mr. Benjamin. Everybody, say hi to Benjamin!" the janitor says, cheerly.

Nobody speaks.

"Of course, we're in a secret meeting, not an AA meeting. Although, I sort of having been drinking a lot recently..."

The sound of a throat clearing, coming from one of the balconies. Benjamin doesn't know which.

"Yes, the matter at hand. We're here to discuss the Monster, the Scourge of the Mall, The Disease. Mr. Benjamin here met him once, in the woman's bathroom down the hall, and so we thought it was fair to bring him up to speed."

"Actually, if I may interrupt, I met with him twice, the second time as the ice cream man," says Benjamin.

"No no, Benji, that wasn't the Monster, just a really frustrated ice cream man. We'll get to him shortly. We need to talk about the Monster."

Benjamin imagines himself nodding, and the janitor acts like he'd noticed it.

"The Monster is an ancient being, born from the remains of a dying funcion. You see, we lie on the critical strip of the Rienmann zeta function. In our reality, there are infinite zeroes here, and they are all probably in the critical line, what we call the Nexus. This Monster has the power to bend reality at its will, to change the nature of the function, thus making appear new non-trivial zeroes outside the critical strip. Whenever this happen, the Nexus corrects reality, by using some symmetry properties not relevant to our discussion. The problem is that the Monster is getting stronger, and once he's able to produce a pseudo-zero lying outside the critical strip, our reality will collapse and everything will cease to exist."

Benjamin can't follow any of it. He once again feels like his inside a dream, like reality means no more than the smile drawn on his face.

"Mr. Janitor, sir, I'm sorry, but I don't understand. I was sucked into a situation I have no control over, and all I want is... I don't even know what I want. I didn't exist before being trapped by Karen, at least I don't remember anything from before. Some noseless girl says I wrote a book, now all this talk of functions and zeroes and critical things. I thought I would come here to be enlightened, not to leave more confused than I already was."

The janitor is not laughing anymore.

"All in due time, Benjamin. You know now that the Monster has an analytical nature, it's all theory. All words and numbers. Absurd, really. The nature of reality is shaped by ink and numeric codes typed into a keyboard. You need to avoid the Nexus, for there you will find substance, the opposite of the Absurd. The Monster is a child of the Absurd, but in the Nexus, there is only truth."

Benjamin commands the Boy to stand up, who obliges.

"If I need to avoid the Nexus, why bring me here in the first place?" says the balloon.

"You're important, Benjamin. You can't not exist, you matter to the Nexus. But you can't reach it, never. We brought you here to tell you that you will be protected. We got your back, and that's all you need to know. The Monster and the aberrations it has spawned, like the ice cream man, will be dealt with. You're free to float around here, basking in the Absurd and all its power. But you can never reach the Nexus. You need to exist, not to act. By existing alone, and never reaching the Nexus, you and I will destroy the Monster, and cure the mall."

At the mention of a cure, Benjamin remembers something.

"I have one memory, or at least I think it's a memory. Something about the soul of the mall, and that is diseased. Your speech reminded me of this. You called the Monster 'the Disease', and now you're talking about a cure. What is the soul of the mall, and why do I remember this?" says Benjamin.

The janitor is clearly upset now.

"The soul of the mall is the Nexus, is just another name for it," says the now sweating janitor.

Benjamin looks at him, and if he could, he would cast a doubtful look at the speaker.

"We're through here. Just remember, Benjamin: Stay away from the Nexus. If the Monster shows itself to you, ignore it. It can't exist without being feared."

He gathers some papers he had put in the podium in front of him.

"This meeting is over."

With that, the four cloaked figures burst into bubbles and float away.

Benjamin, the Boy and the janitor walk up the stairs towards the store. It's daylight again, and the store is open, several customers browse electronic products.

The balloon stops the janitor by the store's front door.

"You never told me what the green men were looking at in here," he says.

"And I never shall. Good day, balloon," says the janitor as he melts away and soaks the floor, flowing through the door and disappearing.

"Let's go, son. To where, I don't know yet," says Benjamin, feeling completely down.

A cloaked hand touches the Boy's shoulder, and he turns around with Benjamin in hand.

"Everything he said is a lie. The Nexus is your destiny, and I'll help you get there," says the voice. Benjamin gasps mentally when he see who it is.

The noseless girl.

"I suppose I shouldn't be surprised to see you here," Benjamin says.

"You shouldn't talk so much, you know? Communication is bad for you."

Benjamin mentally nods at this. He's been feeling as if on a dream more frequently as of late.

"Come with me, there's a movie playing. An adaptation of a book we both know something about," she says, winking. She's his buddy now, it's what her smile says.

"Okay," Benjamin says. "Maybe I can you give that autograph you wanted."

Her smiles widens even more.

Benjamin commands the Boy, and they all head to the movie theater.

The way up to the theater is through a giant anaconda. You need to step on its head, and then it takes you up to the jungle above the mall where the theater is.

"Wait a minute, sometimes the snake is hungry, and it asks for some food," says the girl, petting the giant animal. "He's hungry now, I see," she says.

"Do you have some food?" says Benjamin.

She smiles again, and Benjamin thinks she's very pretty

35

for someone with no nose.

Then she snatches him away from the Boy and jams him into the snake's maw, that closes hard. A pop is heard as Benjamin bursts into air.

"Finally," says the girl, wiping her hands on her black cloak and walking away calmly.

The Boy just stands there as the snake closes its eyes for a post meal nap. He has nowhere else to go.

Chapter Five
When the Postman Killed My Dog: An Excerpt

I woke up thinking I was falling. You know that feeling, when you think you're awake and close to sleep, but you're actually already sleeping and dreaming you're walking, or climbing up stairs, or running. And then you trip, or you lose your step, and you fall in your dream, and you feel it in your chest, and you wake up gasping for air, nervous, trying to catch a step you really never lost.

But in my case, I was actually falling.

I was in a dark tunnel. So dark I couldn't see the walls, couldn't make out the shape. It could be cylindrical, rectangular, you name it. To me, it was a complete void. I tried to scream, but my voice came out high pitched, like I'd just inhaled helium.

Eventually, I quit screaming and just relaxed. There was nothing I could do, no one who could help me. I accepted my fate, and made the most out of it: I took another nap.

Trying to fall asleep while falling through infinity is tough, and I'm proud of myself for actually doing it. My sleep was dreamless this time, and when I woke up, I wasn't falling no more.

The floor I was on was covered in brown leaves. I was in a small cave, big enough to fit me standing up, and there was light enough to see perfectly fine, I just didn't knew where it came from.

After I stood up, I measured it out. It was about ten paces in lenght between each of the opposite walls. It was more like a room carved in solid rock than a cave, really.

Finished assessing my whereabouts, I felt myself for wounds and lacerations, anything. But, aside from a weird bite mark on my neck, I found nothing wrong with me.

Looking down, I saw that I wasn't alone in my prison. A group of ants was passing through, carrying leaves, undoubtdely to their home.

I lay on my chest to look at them, because I thought they seemed odd from afar.

And I was right; they were bright yellow. I picked up one, let it walk through my hand, and rubbed it gently. Its skin was rubbery, like latex. Kind of like a balloon.

I squeezed the ant between two fingers, and it produced a barely audible popping sound.

They actually were balloon ants.

I looked closely to another one, and saw they had no mouth. Instead, they had faces drawn, little tiny smiley faces on their heads.

"What the fuck?" I said.

"Fuck you, asshole, you've just killed my cousin Kyle!"

I wasn't above recognizing an ant had just talked to me. I looked down, and felt my head spinning. I tried to grasp one of the walls for support, but the dizzy spell was a strong one.

When I finally regained my equilibrium after what felt like hours, I looked up and saw the ant standing in my eye level.

The room was now gigantic, and I was somehow reduced to the size of the ants.

"Or maybe everthing else grew," I thought out loud.

"I'm going to show you something big when I shove my ant cock in your asshole, you bastard," the angry ant said.

"Sorry, mate," I said. I was glad my voice was back to normal.

"I didn't mean to kill your relative. I just thought, you know..."

"Yeah, you thought, 'hey, what does another dead ant means, eh? Absolutely nothing!'. Well, I have news for you, he was getting married next week, how do you like that? Do you want to be the one to tell his fiancée at home that you've killed the only man she's ever loved?"

I felt like complete shit.

"Again, I'm sorry, I wasn't thinking straight. I just fell through an infinite hole."

The ant began laughing, a loud and obnoxious sound, but strangely infectious at the same time.

"I'm just fucking with you, man. That guy was just a pedophile. The boss made us work with him because he worked hard, but he was nothing but a larvae fiddler. You did us all a favor."

Soon, I joined the ant in laughter. We both laughed so hard, we inspired the rest of the ants to join in. That's when reality hit and I passed out again.

When I woke up, I was lying down on top of an ant. We were on the move, and the Funny Ant led the way.

"Where are we going? How did we left that room?" I said, still groggy as hell, getting up and riding the ant as a horse. It didn't seemed to mind.

"Ok, two questions were asked, now here's two answers: We're going to see the boss, he's been expecting you for a long time. That's one answer. And the second answer is, we're ants. We can pass through the tinyest holes."

"That's what she said," a new ant said, feeling frisky.

The Funny Ant turned, and although you couldn't tell because of the permanent smile painted on, you could feel the rage.

"Talk out of line again, Angus, and I'll fucking pop you, you hear me?"

Angus retreated back to his place in line, head down.

All the ants were alike; yellow, rubbery and with a smiley face painted on.

"What's your name?" I asked the Funny Ant, clearly the leader.

"Leonhard," he said. "Leonhard, the Funny Ant."

I almost mentioned to him how that was a great coincidence, that I was thinking of him as Funny Ant, but I could still sense some fury in his voice.

Trying to lighten up the mood, I said:

"So, you say your boss has been waiting for me. That means he must know who I am and where I come from, right? Because I sure don't."

"You're the Starman. You have been prophesied millenia ago. Now shut the fuck up, our boss will tell you everything you need to know."

I decided to shut the fuck up as Leonhard the Funny Ant had suggested me.

Time was acting weird during our journey to the ants' home. I saw a small flower on the ground aging from a tiny sprout to the full flower, and then dying, in a matter of seconds. Several stalactites and stalagmites formed and broke off in the time between us first seeing them and right before it was out of our field of vision.

I was still wondering if I had grown smaller of if everything else had grown bigger, but decided against asking Leonhard the Funny Ant about it.

"We're here," one of the ants said as we approached a

large stone gate.

Leonhard the Funny Ant touched his latex head on the gate, and muttered some words. The gate opened slowly, and we passed through it.

Inside, the temperature dropped significantly. I held my ant tighter, being careful as to not pop it. Even so, I felt cold.

The inside of the ants' home seemed to be deserted. It was a big cave, with lots of tunnels dug on its sides. It was wider in the middle, like it was egg shaped. On the center, there was a giant throne, at least for my current size. It was a man's throne.

The ants in my escort began to run wild, breaking formation, inspecting the tunnels.

"What's going on, Leonhard?" I asked.

But Leonhard didn't seem to listen. He was inspecting the base with the other ants. Just my escort remained still.

"What's your name, buddy?" I asked, but got no response. I think he was just as nervous as the rest of them.

"They're gone! They're all gone!" one of the ants said from one of the tunnels.

All of the ants reconvened close to the stone gate. Their smiley painted faces couldn't show their worries, but I could sense it.

Leonhard the Funny Ant was the one who did the talking.

"Alright, men, it has happened. The Monster has attacked. He took our women and our children and our elders. And worst of all, he took our boss away."

Audible gasps from the ants. I don't know how, since they had no mouths, but I took it in stride.

"It's our job now to instruct and prepare the Starman for his fight against the Monster."

He turned to me, and I felt a speech coming. It's funny how sometimes we can do that.

"It's not my job telling you what I'm about to tell you, but the boss is gone and you are only hope, comprende?"

I just nodded, not wanting to interrupt.

"Good. So, thousands of years ago, a man, a woman and their cat found this cave. The woman was pregnant. They build that throne and the first of the ant tunnels, where they lived. They ate moss and some animals that are now long extinct. One day, the man discovered our Sacred Fountain, which I'll show you in a second. The man made us from the Fountain, and we built the tunnels."

"The man's wife gave birth to twin boys. She died during labor, and the man was distraught. He gave his children no name, at least none that were recorded in history."

"Time went by, and the boys grew up. With us, they built other tunnels and caves beyond imagination."

"The man raised them telling him stories about the wasteland that was the surface. He spoke of giant beasts roaming the planet, eating humans, and how the seas were infected with disease and sea monsters so vile, you'd go insane just looking at one."

"One day, one of the boys found something in a cave. It was a Fountain like ours, but it was different. It stenched, and the water was foul. The boy is said to have drank from that dark Fountain, and he became what we now call Monster. His brother tried to stop him, but the Monster fought him, and severely wounded him. The man took his wounded son back to his cave, and collapsed the way to the dark Fountain, trapping the Monster there."

I was hypnotized by the story. Leonhard the Funny Ant had a beautiful speaking voice, and he was on full speech mode.

"Back in our home, the man told us all he was taking his son and his cat back up, to the surface. He knew people who could heal the boy. The man promised one day, a man would come from the stars, and it would be his descendant. That man would destroy the Monster, but until then, the Monster would be the scourge of our land. He left instructions to take the Starman to our Fountain, and there, he would arm himself to destroy the Monster. And before he left, he built our boss, a man made out of the same material as us, and left him in charge of his cave, until the return of his offspring.

Leonhard the Funny Ant finished his speech, and was visibly tired afterwards. I mean, I couldn't see it in his face, but you get the idea.

"Leonhard, I can't be the Starman. I don't even know my name or where I come from. I woke up falling through the hole, and as far as I know, my entire existence began at that moment."

The ants seemed nervous.

"You must be the Starman. You are the only one who fell though the hole in thousands of years, you have been prophesied. What you don't remember doesn't matter. You are here now, and you're going to save us all. Men, take him to the Fountain."

My friend who was carrying me began to move towards the wall opposite the gate. The other ants flanked us, as if worrying I might get off and flee.

To tell you the truth, I was kind of looking forward to it. The thought of suiting up and fighting a terrible Monster felt right to me.

We walked past through the empty cave and arrived at a small opening that lead to a tunnel. We continued through this new tunnel that was inclined, leading us forever down and to the left.

"Prepare yourself, Starman, your time has come," Leonhard the Funny Ant said when we reached our goal.

It was a small cave lit up by the Fountain.

The water was bright yellow. The golden light shone on us, and the ants assumed kind of a reverent posture.

"Stand beneath the waters, Starman. It's time."

I nodded and got off my silent friend. I petted him on his head and marched to the Fountain.

My life began when I was falling through the hole. And at that, I discovered I had a purpose. My life wasn't without meaning.

Leonhard the Funny Ant directed me to the water stream. He told me to stand under the fall and just let the water wash over me.

I did as I was told.

The water initially felt cool and refreshing. I closed my eyes and just enjoyed.

But then, I began feeling a rise in the temperature. Steam began to rise as I stood there, compeltely paralyzed.

The heat became unberable. I screamed as the hot water burned my flesh. Chunks of my skin began to fall off, globs of meat and blood streaking the water red.

My teeth fell off, as did my hair and nails.

The hot water burned a hole through my stomach and my insides were washed out by it.

All the pain should have made me pass out, but I was awake during the whole time.

I could hear the sizzling of my flesh. And when I was no more than a skeleton, the water began to change again. This time, the water was warm and confortable. It wrapped around me, covering my exposed bones and muscle, making me complete again.

The sensation was overwhelming. I was dismantled and now I was being put back together again. I looked at my body, and saw it had become yellow and rubbery, just like the ants.

Steam rose up and entered through my mouth, which was still exposed. I could feel the hot air destroying what was left of me, purging me. Then, it filled me, mantaining shape.

When it was done, more water came and closed my mouth hole.

After I was complete, I stepped out of the water, a new man. The Starman of the prophecy.

My silent friend stepped up. He lifted his foot and drew on my face.

A permanent smile.

"Starman, will you lead us to victory?" Leonhard the Funny Ant said.

I looked at him. I could feel a new life within.

"Yes," I said. My voice was realer now. It was right.

"Then let's go."

He led us back through the tunnel, back to the main cave. We went through a different tunnel. Again, time acted funny. Huge mushrooms sprouted from the ground, and bizarre insects were born and died several times over before we reached our destination: The Monster tunnel.

It was a large stone gate, just like the one at the ants's home.

Except, this one had a rubber coating on it. With a smile painted on.

"The boss..," Leonhard the Funny Ant said.

That was enough to set the ants in war mode. They screeched and scratched at the rocks below.

"Ants, this is the body of your boss. Behind this gate are your people. Will you come with me to destroy the Monster?" I asked.

I screamed.

And they all screamed back, as the gate opened and all light left the world.

45

Chapter Six
Movie Night

"So, how did you like it?" the ice cream man asks.

Benjamin's not sure. He remembers not being anymore, and then being again, sitting in the jungle movie theater, watching an adaptation of *When The Postman Killed My Dog* projected onto two elephants' ears stitched together. All of that in the company of the deranged, giant headed, small bodied ice cream man.

"I thought it was a little bit melodramatic. That whole 'it's my destiny, it's my purpose' theme is not really my thing, I guess. I have existed for very little time by my reference, so I don't really know the full extent of my cultural preferences."

"I kind of like it," says the ice cream man. "I think it shows how one can adapt one's mind to unimaginable situations and still maintain a positive outlook."

Benjamin nods. He's sitting between the ice cream man and the Boy, who has Fred on his lap. Instead of chairs, the movie theater's seats are big turtles adapted with chair backs so the viewers can be confortable.

"I see your point, but I just have one question," says Benjamin. "Why am I wearing a wig?"

And in fact, Benjamin is fitted with a wig of luxurious black hair, long and natural looking, no heavy styling needed. The ice cream man turns to him and smiles. Not an overtly creepy, evil smile, like when he was trying to get Benjamin to eat the ice cream, but a more gentle one.

"Sorry about that. It's just the thought of going out on a movie date with a beautiful woman kind of excites me. It's been a long time since..."

Benjamin feels bad for the man.

"Okay, I can understand that. It's just... I'm not confortable being like this, so vulnerable. Especially since you tried to steal my juices."

This time, the ice cream man lets out a hearty laugh. Other people in the theater would shush him, if there were any other people present. Apparently. *When The Postman Killed My Dog: The Movie* is a big box office flop.

"Don't worry about that, amigo. The Nexus is permanently closed to me. I will never reach it, so we're just here enjoying a movie."

The movie ended right after the man became a balloon, but that didn't seemed right to Benjamin. Where is the battle, the redemption of the ants?

"I just don't understand the ending. There should be more than just this," says the balloon.

"That's what we all say. The great axiom is 'There should be more than this'," says the ice cream man, with a dreamy voice.

Benjamin has no answer for that.

"Well, it's time to go," says the ice cream man, getting up from his turtle. "The movie is over."

"Wait!" says Benjamin, as the Boy gets up and grabs his string, throwing the wig from the top of the balloon's head on the floor. Fred scurries off into the jungle before the Boy can grab him.

"The Nexus. Everybody has its own definition. I can't fully grasp its meaning, so I ask you: What is the Nexus?."

The ice cream produces an empty cone from his pocket.

"You know that question you had about the movie? The 'there's should be more than this' bit? The Nexus is more than this," he says, waving his arms, indicating the junglescape

47

around them.

"I don't understand," says Benjamin.

"It's alright, nobody does," says the ice cream. He throws the cone up, and his body liquefies and turns into creamy Passion Fruit Delight. The mass of ice cream flows upwards and intercepts the cone, filling it, before it lands on the floor and breaks, spreading sweet yellow goo all around.

"Let's go, son," says the ballon, and they both walk out of the theater, towards the anaconda elevator.

"I hope it's not hungry right now," thinks Benjamin.

It isn't, and it takes them down to the mall with quickness and ease.

Benjamin turns and commands the Boy to pet the head of the snake, as a thank you sign.

"Don't push it, freak," says the snake, and Benjamin and the Boy walk away.

It's nighttime, and the mall is closed.

They walk down the shutdown escalators and arrive at the mall's lobby.

The whole first floor is the body of a dead god, a nameless being that fell from the skies millions of years ago. The body decayed, leaving only isolated lumps of flesh that were carved out and served as stores, and the negative space became hallways and passageways. The center of the lobby is right where the beast's heart would have been, and an artificial fountain was built to pretty things up.

The Boy sits by the fountain, and Benjamin reflects on the past events.

"It's nice to have this time for ourselves, especially since everytime we're out of a situation, we're right back into another one. That's a lot of missing time between scenes, and we need to try to fill those out with memories."

The Boy lets his hand drift through the water.

"I remember the noseless girl's betrayal, and then I was in the movie theater wearing a wig and sitting beside the ice cream man. But I can't fill in the missing time in between, and I feel that's necessary to fight the Monster. I need to remember before the final battle that is surely coming."

"I need to make use of this time right now, just you and me. I need your help, son. Back at the ice cream stand, I thought I heard you saying something. It was a sound unlike any other I've ever heard. I think that was you. Do you think you can talk to me? Now it's the time.

The Boy says nothing. He just brushes his hand in the water.

Benjamin is disappointed. At the same time he senses he possess great knowledge and power, but can't access it. He feels locked inside his own latex skin.

"Maybe we need to go away. Just leave this place behind, start a new life somewhere, what do you think?"

The Boy takes his hand of the water and stands up. He seems pleased by the idea.

He grabs Benjamin without a command and runs towards the wide mall doors.

"Wait!" Benjamin says.

They stop by the glass exit doors, and Benjamin has a chance to inspect the world outside.It's all pitch black. The easiest things to see are the signs of destruction, and only when the land is lit up by violent lightning. It's a desert of chaos and death.

Benjamin sees bodies scattered close to the doors, long decomposed. Some are still clutching shopping bags.

"I guess we're stuck here, son. Let's go upstairs, maybe we can find my book in Karen's store."

He does not move.

"Son, lets's go."

49

The Boy slams his fists hard on the doors. Once, twice, three times.

Benjamin can feel the frustration emanating from the heavy set headless kid.

"I know, I wanted it out too, son, but we can't go. We need to sort this out before we leave."

They turn around, and see globs of the god's flesh scurrying from the stores and gathering by the fountain.

"Are you going to give up that easily, balloon? How do you know that what you're seeing outside isn't one of my delightful pranks?" says a voice coming from above.

"Not now," thinks Benjamin. "We're not ready."

"Ooooh, the balloonny is scared. You're just doggy doodoo sprinkled on a doggy doodoo sandwich! You're the one who raped my mother and killed my grandfather! You're fucking lung cancer!"

The Monster does not show himself. He speaks as a pure disenbodied voice. Meanwhile, the pieces of flesh begin to merge and shape themselves, until they become green men.

"Die, doggy doodoo!" screamed the Monster's voice, as the green men charged.

"I don't think help is coming, son, brace yourself."

But instead, the Boy ties Benjamin's string to the door, and charges back at the green men.

There are six of them total, and the Boy is pure rage. He throws his fists at them, beating them up, smashing heads together. They try to hurt him, but their blows do nothing more than to anger the headless beast. He rips of arms, crushes two of them together until the sound of bones cracking can be heard, he steps on a fallen green man's skull and it shatters under his mighty feet.

"No, no!" says the Monster. He conjures up more green men, who ignore the Boy and go straight to Benjamin.

The Boy is held by more of the green men, who grab him by every member. But as he sees more of them rushing towards Benjamin, he shakes off the ones holding on to him and charges.

Before the first green men can put their disgusting hands on Benjamin, the Boy is there, kicking the green man so hard on his back, he's launched through the glass door, breaking it. The sounds of beasts devouring the green man can be heard from within the mall.

"You fool, you can't fuck with that glass!" says the Monster, as he bends reality and fixes the door.

Benjamin notices this and has a plan, which he conveys to the Boy.

Knowing what to do, the Boy grabs more green men and throws them out the glass. He beats one with his own ripped off arm, and uses the limb as a bat, hitting the man so hard, his head flies out like a cannonball and breaks another section of the glass.

Soon, all of the green men are either dead or agonizing on the other side of the doors, and more and more beasts gather up to their unexpected feast.

Benjamin is not sure he can see the animals, but he's pretty sure at least one is a rabid, feral dog wearing a postman's hat.

"You fuckers, you broke my toys again! I hate you and I hope you get cooties!" says the Monster's voice, and then it's no more.

Benjamin commands the Boy to get some wood in a nearby hardware store, to board up the patches of broken glass. He obeys, but he's visibly tired. Benjamin tries to pass along some energy, because the task seems imperative. As the Monster, he too is afraid of the wild beasts that roam the wasteland.

When the task is done, the Boy collapses by the Fountain. Benjamin commands only his hand to grab some water and splash on his headless hole, in hopes of cooling off the tired Boy.

Fred comes running from some unknown hideout and licks the Boy's hand.

"You did great, son. We need to harness your anger, our anger, and defeat the Monster. If neither the janitor or the noseless girll will help us, then we'll help ourselves."

The Boy says nothing, just breathes heavily, his chest painfully moving up and down in irregular movements.

"Rest, son. I feel another fade out coming. We need to concentrate, to maintain our memories of the time between the scenes. We need to, we need to..."

And with that, the scene ends.

Chapter Seven
Old Friends

Benjamin and the Boy wander through the empty mall.

All the stores are destroyed, some overgrown with vegetation.

They sit under the Security Guard Tree, and watch some animals passing by. They come from the jungle above, the one that used to house the movie theater.

Some elephants walk by, and Benjamin wonders if the pair that acted as the movie screen was with them. "No, they can't be, a lot of time has passed," thinks Benjamin. And, from the looks of the enviroment around him, he's right.

The appearance of the stores, the hallways, it's like they were abandoned millenia ago. The concrete crumbles apart with any strong wind, the glass is stained and cracked. Some trees are so massive they stand from the bottom floor to the movie theater, their leaves breaking through, acting as death traps to the animals above, who step on them thinking it to be safe ground, and then fall to their deaths.

"Looks like we're all that's left, son," Benjamin says. "I think we may start – wait, what's that?"

One of the round red fruits from the Security Guard Tree grows legs and falls, doing a backflip in the air and landing on its newly acquired feet.

Benjamin has the Boy bringing him near the fruit, who's in the process of growing tiny arms, eyes and a long thin mouth. Its lips are pitch black.

"What day is it?" asks the fruit, its voice very feminine.

"I don't know," says Benjamin, who feels a sharp pain.

He commands the Boy to let go of his string, and floats aimsly until he hits the tree and gets stuck beneath a leaf.

"What is this?" he thinks, the pain emanating from nowhere in particular.

"Today is the 36th," says the fruit. "Everything begins again."

Benjamin still feels pain. The fruit begins moving around the tree, circling it.

"Sheets and quilts will meet again," it says.

The Boy picks Benjamin up, and the a feeling of chubby hand on the string makes Benjamin cry out in the Boy's mind.

"Please, son, let go, I can't, I never felt pain before, make it go away."

Benjamin realizes how dependant he is of the Boy. He has never felt so impotent in his life.

The Boy caresses the balloon's latex body. It soothes Benjamin, takes some of the pain from his mind.

Both the Boy and Benjamin hear a light tap. Someone is coming. And the fruit is still circling the tree.

"Forget about it, don't think anymore," it says.

The tapping grows louder. Benjamin knows both he and the Boy are not up for another battle, not yet.

Benjamin looks towards the darkened mall, towards the tapping, and he sees from where the sound is coming from.

It's Fred.

The cat is now old, ancient. He walks on two legs, and uses a cane. He has a man's mustache and wears a Fedora, the same one Karen has put on Benjamin's head.

Benjamin smiles inside. The pain still lingers, albeit not as strong, but he can feel happiness coming from the Boy.

"You can let me go, son. Go to him"

The Boy gently puts Benjamin agains the tree, being

careful as not to put him in the way of the fruit, and goes to the aging cat.

He hugs Fred, with extra care, as to not hurt his old bones, and brings him close to Benjamin.

"How did you manage to last so long, Fred? At least a thousand years has passed."

Fred is staring at the fruit.

"Blue scarf, tightening, whitening, your thinking."

The cat rubs itself against Benjamin, who's not worried. He knows the cat would never hurt him.

Then, Fred takes a single leap and bites the fruit, taking a big chunk of its head. One of its eyes is missing, and a green sludge gushes from the bite site.

"Forget about it?" it says, its feminine voice sounding distorted, as if it were an anonymous witness giving an interview. Then it dies.

Benjamin watches as Fred licks the ooze from the floor, lapping all of it.

"Fred...," Benjamin begins to say.

"Oh hi, Benji," says Fred. His voice is very familiar to the balloon.

"I know you," Benjamin says.

"Of course, darling, I'm your wife!"

It is Karen. Her voice is coming from the elderly cat.

Benjamin can finally communicate with Karen. He tried to save her, warn her of the green men, but no contact was allowed between them.

"I'm sorry, Karen," Benjamin says.

"Sorry for what? I just woke up from a long nap, that's it."

Karen/Fred circles the tree, looking up at the other red fruits.

"They sure are yummy, hunny," she says, and giggles when it rhymes.

"I'll cook us some for dinner, how about it? I'm sure Junior would love it."

Benjamin looks at the Boy, and sees that a fruit has landed on his head hole. The fruit was changing in front of Benjamin's eyes. It was shaping itself like a human head, growing in size, and sprouting eyes, nose, lips, ears, hair, mouth. All of it was red.

Meanwhile, Benjamin sees that the body of Fred is also going through metamorphosis. His jaws are completely open in an obtuse angle, gradualy opening more and more. His insides are moving through his body and exiting though the gaping hole. The viscera begins to form a new shape, and Benjamin realised in terror that it is a human body.

The guts are shaping up to be Karen.

Benjamin focuses in on his pain. He perceives it as a breakthrough, as something pushing him closer to the ultimate truth.

He concentrates on the top of the Security Guard Tree, willing himself up. He can feel something changing, he does not feel as if on a dream anymore.

The grotesque caricatures continue their transformations, the Boy now aware of the parasite on his head place. He punches it, trying to knock it out before it is complete.

And the Karen made of viscera is already as tall as the original bookeeper, and it's now just refining the shape to match hers.

"Please!" Benjamin screams.

He feels himself being pushed upwards. He's drifting now, with a purpose, not aimsly. He feels like he's controlling everything, as if he knows everything about anything.

He passes by the Boy, and is able to coil his string on the fruit face. Cherishing the help, the Boy falls back while the face is tied by Benjamin. The fruit gets tangled on the balloon's string, and head and body are separated.

Howling in pain, the fruit begins to sizzle and melt, letting out a disgusting odor.

The viscera Karen also feels something.

"No, Benji, come back!" it screams, the voice even more distorted.

"I love y-." Its speech is cut off when it explodes, smearing blood and guts all over the base of the tree, and on the Boy's body.

Benjamin continues his ascent, and during that he sees Fred, the real, young Fred, emerging from the old cat cocoon that house the fake Karen. He sees as the cat goes up to the Boy and licks his face, snuggling against his collapsed body.

"Thank you, Fred, for taking care of my boy while I'm away."

The ascent seems to last forever. The tree is a lot taller than Benjamin remembered.

After what it seemed like years, Benjamin arrives at the top, and finds the ice cream man sitting on a large leaf.

"We're not in the mall anymore, are we?" says Benjamin, as the ice cream man picks up his string and pulls him closer."

"No," says the man.

"Is this the Nexus?" says Benjamin.

The ice cream looks at the balloon. He looks tired, his mustache has disappeared, the muscle tone in his head looks weaker, like he's aged as well.

"No. There is no more Nexus, it's gone. The Monster won, reality has ceased to exist. Look."

Benjamin looks down, and sees all white. The tree is the only thing that has left in the Universe.

"I see," the balloon says, fighting the sadness away. He already misses the Boy. "And what now?"

"Now, we wait for the end. I have some ice cream here

with me, do you want some? It's Passion Fruit Delight."

Benjamin thinks of his first encounter with the ice cream man. He seemed so desperate for him to eat the ice cream.

"I feel like this is a trap," Benjamin says.

The ice cream man attempts a feeble smile.

"No more traps, amigo. I'm all tapped out. Everything is gone now. There's a non trivial zero of the Rienmann zeta function that lies outside the critical strip. There is no god."

Benjamin looks at the man. He can see he's dying, his head is pulsating in a strange rhythm.

"I don't think there ever was a god," says the balloon.

The ice cream man looks shocked at this.

"There was, Mr. Balloon. He was in the Nexus, I've met him before he was sent there."

"How was he like?" asks Benjamin.

"I can't remember. Even memory can't survive the desecration of the Rienman zeta function. All I know is that we are both here, and that we should enjoy some ice cream together."

Benjamin sighs in his mind.

"Ok, Mr. Dastardly," says Benjamin. "Let me have some of that sugary goodness."

The ice cream man pulls a cone from his cooler and brings it close to Benjamin's face. A purple-ish light appears, circling Benjamin. They both watch as the ice cream is pulled towards the light, and disappears.

"Hummm, that's very good!" says Benjamin, feeling completely happy and refreshed.

After a few seconds, the light reappears and begins to spew out disgusting yellow vomit.

"That's REALLY good!" screams Benjamin.

The ice cream man is now just a skeleton holding up the cone.

"More, more!" Benjamin says. He's completely frantic.

The cone itself is sucked towards Benjamin's insides, and it's destroyed by the event horizon.

"I feel alive for the first time," the balloon says, as the cooler, the leaves, and the very body of the ice cream man are sucked into him.

Now, it's only Benjamin and the yellow bile, floating in front of him in a pool of whiteness.

"I can see it," says the balloon. "I know what to do now"

Sugar is known to have this sort of effect on balloons.

Benjamin floats towards the vomit. He inspects it with his newly found mind's eye.

"I'm coming for you," Benjamin says.

And he absorbs the vomit back to him. When the bile hits the event horizon, a large puple explosion occurs, all the whiteness melts away, and construction of a new reality begins.

"Today *is* the 36th. Everything begins again," says the balloon, as the vomit breaks through the event horizon, causing Existence to phase out, and then phase back in again.

Chapter Eight
The Problem
with Communication

The feeling of falling is something new to Benjamin. As a balloon, he's not used to be affected by things like weight and gravity.

But now he feels it; he feels the air rushing by him, feels the shift in position.

"I'm in between phases. Existence is blinking, I just need it to open its eyes," thinks Benjamin. And the the rushing stops.

He's in a large library. Shelves of books extend as far as the eye can see, parallel to each other. It's a giant hallway of books.

"Who are you?" asks a voice.

Benjamin turns around and sees a skinny man sitting in a lounge chair by a shelf. He has a long black beard, and is wearing torn jeans and no shirt. He's very white and pale, and has multiple veins visible through his skin.

"I am Benjamin," says the balloon.

The man is holding up a book. He looks at Benjamin, then starts looking for a specific page. When he finds it, he reads from it.

"Don't spoil it for me, I'm not there yet!" the man says.

Benjamin moves closer to the man. He reads the title on the book.

When The Postman Killed My Dog.

The shock washes over Benjamin. He finally realizes

that he's moving by himself.

He looks down and sees he has arms and legs, made of string. They are extremely thin, just white lines holding him up. He's a stick figure made of string, with a balloon head.

"What happened?" he says. He's panicking.

"Damn it, I didn't knew you'd be like this, now you've done and ruined it!" says the man, visibly angry, throwing the book on the floor.

Benjamin bends down and picks the book up.

"I've been looking everywhere for this," says Benjamin, almost crying.

"It's not very good," says the man. "It's very melodramatic. Not exactly my cup of tea. I'm more of a literary fiction kind of guy." And he laughs.

Ignoring the man, Benjamin leafs through the book. He recognizes the movie he saw with the ice cream man, but that's only half the book.

The second half is missing.

Benjamin turns towards the man, who continues laughing maniacally.

"Where is the rest? Where is it?!" Benjamin says. He imagines his smiling face turning angry, turning desperate.

The man composes himself from his insane laughter.

"I told you, man, I'm not there yet. As I read it, the book opens up to me. Without me reading it, it's nothing."

Benjamin marches (something he never thought he could ever do) and grabs the man with his string arms, coiling them around the man's wrists.

"Read it then! Read it, I need to know about it, I need to know about the Nexus!"

The man keeps calm during Benjamin's outburst.

"We're in it, man. This is the Nexus," says the man, straightening out his jeans after Benjamin releases him.

The balloon stumbles back. He sees the infinite lines of books forming a hallways that goes on forever.

"So, did the Monster actually win? Is the Universe over?"

Picking his book up from the floor, the man smiles at Benjamin.

"I don't know. I need to finish reading the book, I need to know if this is the book I'm looking for."

Benjamin says nothing, only keeps on staring at the endless books.

"You see, I'm trapped here for millions of years. Billions maybe. I come from a once great realm, filled with different people, different races and religions."

The man puts the book back in its place in the shelf.

"There, I'll finish you later. So, where was I?" says the man.

"You were about to launch in one more meaningless speech, just like the ones I already listened to," says Benjamin, without diverting his eyes from the hallway.

"Right! My people became obsessed with this one book. I never knew its name, since at the time I was exiled due to illness.

Benjamin turns to the man. He didn't look sick at all.

"And then what?" says the balloon.

"They all jumped in. They entered the book and then all reality got screwed up. I was sucked from my prison hospital to this place. I just need to find the book and then I'm off to the good times with my peeps!"

The man starts jumping around, dancing to a song only he can hear. Benjamin can see the man has become insane after the millions of years in the Nexus.

"Tell me, friend," says Benjamin, calmer now. "What do you know about this place?"

Interrupting his dance, the man becomes more serious.

He stares into Benjamin's painted on eyes.

"This is an unstable place. There shouldn't be more than one person here, really. You being here messes things up. And besides, you're spoiling the book for me."

"How am I spoiling it? How would you know that?" says Benjamin. The quantity of information is overwhelming.

"You're giving it all away! I'm reading about a balloon man, with normal, albeit balloony, limbs, and suddenly you appear, all stringy and skinny. It's obvious you've been blown up, except for your head. I was dying to know how the battle with the Monster went!"

Benjamin hears a rustling noise from behind a close shelf.

"Oh shit, the bookmites," says the man.

"For your tone, I take that is a bad thing," says Benjamin.

"Yeah, no shit. They guard this place. They don't like people here."

"How do you deal with them?"

The man sits on the floor.

"I usually just read them a story, and they keep to themselves."

Benjamin is in the Nexus. He's finally reached the place everyone was talking about. And it's a hallway full of bookshelves.

"This can't be it."

"What's that?" the man says. He's picking dirt from his toenails.

"I said this can't be it," says Benjamin. "I did not lose my only friend and my reality for this."

"Well, what did you expect from a graph? Math is fucked up that way."

Benjamin looks at the man.

"Fuck math," he says.

"YEAH, fuck math, balloon homie!" says the man. "That's a great nickname, though... balloon homie. I'll call you ballomie"

Benjamin walks up to the seated man. He extendes his stringed arms and wraps them around the man's neck.

"Fuck you!" he screams, choking the life from his victim.

The man tugs at Benjamin's arms, his eyes bulging and his face turning purple. The balloon doesn't let go. He's now mad with information, his senses had turned against him. Finally he understood just how fucked up communication was.

"I want it, the feeling. I want to feel your life leaving you," says the deranged balloon.

The man, sensing he's about to lose consciousness, reach out and grab a random book from the nearest shelf. He opens the book one-handed, and positions it above the balloon's head.

Initially, Benjamin only feels a weak tug. Then a stronger one. And then a stronger one. Until the pull becomes so strong, it desintegrates him, reorgazining his molecules onto the pages.

The man breathes with difficulty as he closes the book and puts it back on the shelf.

"Now, where was I," he says, as he picks up *When The Postman Killed My Dog* to finally find out how does it end.

***

Words.
    Characters.
    Punctuation.
    Sentences.
    Periods.

Paragraphs.

All rush past Benjamin as he sails through the pages completely out of control.

The ink rubs against the latex, and he feels the smudges on his head.

He always saw himself as two dimensional, a being born out of nothingness, destined to be forgotten. Now, he can see he was wrong. Now, he is truly two dimensional, and the feeling is like a sword cutting through his existence.

Only small snippets of information can be picked up. Benjamin can't even tell what the book's about.

He lets go, just lets himself be washed by the word waves. He drifts towards something he can't really see, but can imagine what it is: The center of the book, where the pages meet.

A sort of Nexus, really.

Not even thinking about the Nexus can make Benjamin angry. He's completely resigned to his fate, whichever it may be.

"All I want is peace," thinks the balloon, as he surfs the page.

But one word catches Benjamin's eye.

Karen.

Benjamin knows that Karen is a common name. But he can't help feeling being intrigued.

Several other familiar terms rush by.

Balloon. Green Men. Ice Cream. Janitor.

The Boy.

Benjamin was in his own story.

He can see the Nexus clearly now, a black abyss dividing the pages. The book is close, but there is still space between each page, and Benjamin knows the Nexus will either propel him to the opposite page, or suck him into another realm.

As he approaches the Nexus, he sees new words and sentences, ones that he knows nothing about.

Corruption of the Soul.

A desert of insanity.

The beasts feed on the Boy's carcass.

The end.

The pages are shifting beneath Benjamin, showing him what will happen.

He can't let it end like that. He feels the end is near, yes, but he'll be the one writing it.

The Nexus is only seconds away now. Benjamin prepares himself for whatever comes next, and thinks of the Boy.

"I never should have left you down there, son. I just needed to know," he thinks, as he plunges deep into the dark abyss.

***

A dark room. Some chairs are spread out. In the four walls, there are balconies slightly elevated.

It's the secret meeting room.

"Glad you could join us," says a voice. Benjamin looks towards it, and sees a cloaked figure.

The voice is masculine and smooth, unlike the janitor's, and especially unlike the noseless girl's.

"Show yourself," says Benajmin. He's again just a balloon on a string, his new body is gone.

"Gladly," says the voice. "But I should warn you, once I reveal who I am, there's no going back. You still have a chance to leave all this talk of Nexus, souls, funcions, headless people, snakes, janitors and toilets behind. Are you sure you don't want to take it?

Benjamin needs only a second to answer.

"I need to know. The Absurd has won, I'm now his servant."

"You're nobody's servant," says another voice coming from behind Benjamin. He turns and sees the noseless girl, in her own cloak, without the hood.

"I won't believe your lies again, *friend*," says Benjamin.

The girl just smiles, the same devilish smile she always displays to Benjamin.

"She's not lying, Benji, not this time," says another voice, coming from Benjamin's left.

It's Karen, in a black cloak, apparently unharmed.

"Karen, I... I'm sorry. I'm sorry the green men took you, I know how much you cared for me, for the memory of your husband."

"You bear his name, that's right, but I'm not the one who named you. I was disturbed for a while, but now I see the truth."

"Yeah, alls of us see it now, b'loony." A third voice. The security guard comes in, wearing a matching cloak, his canary with the booming speaking voice on his shoulder.

"I see you're ok, Mr. Vinogradov, I'm glad," says Benjamin.

"Livin' as a tree was alrite, lad, but give me a fat belly and my pal canary here and I'm a happy man."

Benjamin was now surrounded by the three figures. The fourth one, the one he first encoutered, has disappeared.

"Where is he? Where is the fouth one?" Benjamin asks. Without the Boy or his stringy body, he is nothing more than a floating head.

"I'm here," says the voice, from atop one of the balconies.

"It's time for the final battle, Benjamin. The Monster has grown too strong. You managed to blink reality out of phase and then bring it back again, but there are no more outs possible. You need to destroy it," says the man, lifting the hood from his face.

Benjamin feels happiness for the first time in a while, as the hood reveals no head at all.

"Son... I'm so sorry."

The Boy looks down on Benjamin from his balcony. Then, he bursts into millions of flying insects, the wings producing a flurry sound Benjamin recognizes.

The insects fly down and reassemble as the Boy in front of Benjamin.

"Benjamin, there is hope. But we need to work together. Are you ready, Benjamin?" asks the Boy, and the balloon has no words. He knows its absurd, that the Boy couldn't be the fourth cloaked figure, that he was with him during the first meeting, but he doesn't care. Even being nobody's servant, Benjamin was right: The Absurd had won. He only nods, the best he can.

"Good," says the Boy. He picks up Benjamin with his two hands, and turn him, making the balloon to look away.

"Now, we'll become what the Monster always feared," says the Boy.

He places Benjamin over his headless hole. The balloon's string gains life on its own, and reaches down and connects with the Boy's inner organs, with his spinal cord.

The Boy gently places Benjamin down as the string acts as the connection.

"This is all I ever wanted," says Benjamin. "To not feel so alone."

A bright light fills the room, as a new being is born.

Chapter Nine
The Beginning of the End

The mall had become a wasteland.

Stores lie broken, the giant's remains are completely decayed now. Green goo cover whatever structure remains standing.

Holes in the walls let in a red, toxic sunlight, that burns any flesh on its path. The glass doors are cracked, and wild beasts gather close to them, waiting for the time they'll be so weak, a simple foot stomp will break them, allowing them the feast they've been waiting for so long.

The new Being, born from the fusion of the Boy and Benjamin, walks through the desolation. It stops to pick up a handful of dirt, and smells it. Eats some of it.

"He's been through here," it says. Its voice is unlike any sound ever produced in the Universe since the beginning of time.

Small furry animals scatter when the Being passes by them. They can sense that it doesn't belong in this Universe. Maybe in none.

"Come on, Monster," says the Being. "Come and play with me."

A gush of wind. The small furry animals retreat back to their burrows, knowing what it means.

"Well well, look what the diseased cat dragged in," says the disenbodied voice of the Monster.

"Speaking of cat, where's the cat-who-is-not-Patty? Oh

yeah, I ate him! HAHAHAHAHAHAHAHAHAHA, he's DEAD!"

"Show yourself, stand before me, and receive your punishment," says the Being, bright light engulfing it, creating a regal armor, protecting it.

"Oooo, baby, what a charming man! Has nature made a man out of you yet?" And the Monster laughs some more.

The bright light around the Being focus in on its hands. A blazing sword and a shining shield appear, the Being ready for war.

"Let's go," says the Being, as it suddenly jumps towards the second floor, a might inhuman jump, and slices through the air.

"AHHHHHHHHHH!" says the Monster, as the sword cuts through.

"How did you know? How *could* you know?" says the wounded demon.

"I can see you,"says the Being, looking straight at the Monster now, a shapeless cloud of darkness. "I can see between the dimensions, where you like to hide. You can't run from me now."

As the Being prepares himself for another blow, the dark cloud vanishes.

"But you still need to find me before you can see me, freak!" yells the Monster, moving so fast the Being can hear the air swooshing.

The Being jumps around slicing the air, extremely fast, but not as fast as the Monster. It tires himself after so many fruitless blows.

It falls back down, panting, its balloon head expanding with each difficult breath.

"Peekabo, motherfucker," says the Monster, now in his man form, as he hugs the Being from behind and flies upwards.

"I'll take you to my place for some drinks, and some DEATH!" he says, flying backwards to the woman's bathroom, taking them both to the toilet realm.

***

The foul stench of the bathroom is replaced by the foul stench of the toilet realm.

It is a place of death and agony. A large tubular place, a wide cylinder that extends infinitely upwards and downwards. Its walls are slimy, and they look like an intestine. The walls are a littered with people, trapped, embedded in the walls, suffering from the sting of scorpions made of feces and liquid urine bees.

Menstrual monsters roam the walls, their dark blood bodies shaped like dictators carrying tridents.

As it's pulled down by the Monster, unable to escape his embrace, the Being watches a Hitler blood ogre stab repetedly a woman in the head. It's Karen.

Each time the Hitler stabs her, the wound heals, so as to receive another piercing of the weapon.

"Looky looky, Mr. Spooky, how do you like my humble abode?" says the Monster, laughing. Although he's still wearing the suit and his shape is vaguely humanoid, he doesn't resemble a human anymore. His face is the same color and texture of the realm's walls, he has four eyes scattered without symmetry and his hands are octopi, each with a will of its own.

"I...don't like it," says the Being. Its voice in this realm is different, more like Benjamin's was. But it don't come out of its mouth only. The Being's voice emanates from the walls, from the mouths of each damned.

71

"No, no, no, what are you doing with my pets? Stop that!" says the Monster.

"I guess I should take you to detention," it says, changing the course of its flight, piercing through one of the walls, taking the head of a damned on with them. The head promply grows back, to continue experiencing torture by the hands of bloody Mussolinis and Pinochets.

The Monster takes them through a tunnel and into a large chamber. At its center, a bloody lake. On one end of the lake, there's a pulpit, and besides it, there's a rectangular table with three seats placed.

"Here you go!" says the Monster, releasing the Being into the lake. The blood is thick and binds the Being in its place, facing towards the pulpit.

The Monster takes his place behind the pulpit.

"Hallelujar, hallelujar! Lawdy, strike down this here sinner, maketh him Your bitch! Gape his asshole with Your Almighty Cock!"

"Here, here!" some voices say.

The Being looks at the table and sees Karen, Mr. Vinogradov with his canary and the Noseless Girl sitting at the table, tied up and being prodded by a man standing on the table with a pitchfork.

"I should have known," says the Being.

The Janitor pokes the prisoners some more, and the Being notices they each have a script in front of them.

"How are you doing, Benjamin?" says the Janitor. "Oh, sorry, you're not Benjamin anymore. I see you let the Absurd make you its bitch. Congratulations, asshole," he says, as he jams the pitchfork in the security guard's head.

The Being doesn't react. He focuses only on the Monster, who watches with glee from his pulpit.

"Are you not entertained, freak?!" says the Monster,

clapping and cheering the Janitor on. "Do it again!" he screams.

The Janitor smiles as he pulls his pitchfork from Mr. Vinogradov's head, ripping it apart as he does it, the fat guard's skull crackling as the blade is pulled out. Blood pours out, and small mushrooms sprout from it.

He walks up to the noseless girl, who's crying.

"Read it," he says.

She just keeps on crying.

"Read it, bitch!" the deranged Janitor says.

"Give it up, freak," she says, sobbing in between every word. "You can't win against the Mighty Monster and his Marvelous Men." The crying overtakes her, and she can't read anymore. She bows her head and sobs.

"Do it!" says the Monster.

"I always hated your face, cunt. It's time for a nose job," the Janitor says, positioning himself behind the girl and then jamming the pitchfork through the back of her head, the middle fork taking the place of a nose, the other two ripping through her cheekbone.

The Being says nothing as the girl's body convulses, and she dies with the blades still inside her. Her blood is blue, and birds emerge from it as it seeps in the table, flying away to their freedom.

"Just one more, asshole, and the Nexus will be finally mine! Janitor, kill the bookworm," the Monster says, literally licking his lips in anticipation.

"My pleasure!" the Janitor says. He walks up to Karen, who's not crying at all, but looking defiantly at her executioner.

"Read it," he says.

"Don't bother, traitor. Just fucking do it."

"I said read it, you -"

73

But before he can finish it, the Being opens his latex mouth. Since his fusion, his face, albeit still being made of rubber, is fully functional.

The sound that comes from the Being's mouth is the mourning of a thousand Universes.

"Oh fuck, what's that?!" screams the Monster, the sound making him cringe, forcing him to cover his ears. It has the same effect on the Janitor, who drops his pitchfork.

They can all see something materializing in the sound. The sound is creating life, new life.

When the Being closes his mouth, its creation lies before the Monster's pulpit.

It's a white cat with a pink bow on it.

"Patty?" says the Monster.

"Yes, I am her," says Patty, the cat. Her voice is that of a really coarse old woman, or a drag queen.

The Monster looks at his childhood pet and begins to cry.

He sits on the floor and cries profusely, hugging his legs close to his body.

The damned souls outside the chamber can hear him crying.

"Why did you leave me, Patty? I loved you," the Monster says, still sobbing.

"You were weak. You're *still* weak. I hate you, Toilet Monster. I hate you," the cat says.

The Monster can't take so much hate from something that used to be an object of affection. He flies out of the chamber, towards the main tunnel.

"Get back here, your fool! It's a trap!" screams the Janitor.

But the Monster is already gone.

"It's useless," says Patty the cat.

She begins to shine, a light so bright it blinds the Janitor.

The sound that made her starts again, and the light shoots through her towards the Being.

"What....," says the Janitor.

The light creates a bridge between Patty and the Being. The shine is too bright, and the Janitor covers his eyes.

When he opens them, he sees the Being standing where Patty used to be, the blood lake empty.

"It's your turn," says the Being, as it marches towards the Janitor.

"The Monster is the master of this realm, but I'm stronger than him, freak," the Janitor says, as he throws his pitchfork in the air. The blades pierce the chamber's soft walls, causing the whole room to shake.

The Being loses its balance, and falls down, giving the Janitor time to flee through a secret opening.

"Die, balloon. It's better for you to die here than trying to face me in our Universe," he says, disappearing through the opening.

"This ends here," says the Being.

It stands up and looks at the pitchfork. The room is colapsing.

The Being runs towards the opening.

"Wait, Benji!" says Karen, still tied to her chair.

"Save me," she says.

The room colapses on her, smashing her completely, spurting blood on the Being's pants. Small green flowers sprout in the fabric, and the Being watches as they grow old and die in a matter of seconds. He then brushes them away, cleaning himself.

"You could have saved her," says a booming voice. The security guard's canary hovers near the Being.

"I know," it says.

"So why didn't you?" the bird asks.

"It's not relevant to the story. Her death was scripted."

The canary flies at the Being's eye level.

"You're bringing corruption to the soul of the mall, you know that, right? You're destroying the Nexus."

"Exactly," says the Being, as it walks slowly away, through the opening, towards the conclusion.

Chapter Ten
Conclusion

The Being escapes the Monster's toilet realm by climbing the tunnel walls.

The tunnel itself is collapsing, big pieces of disgusting material fall past the Being, some still full of damned souls and blood dictators.

It grabs onto the bodies of the damned, embeded in the walls, and pushes itself forever upwards, towards the bowl.

"Please Benji, take us with you," says Karen, already another soul in the wall, as the Being grabs on to her face, ripping chunks of hair and skin as it propels itself.

The Being says nothing. All that is written must take place.

Its ascent is cut short by a bloody Mussolini.

"Your time has come, capisce?" says the fake Duce, as he brings down his hammer on the Being.

The weapon connects with the Being's balloon head, exploding it.

"HAHAHAHAHA, I did it! Master, come back, the balloon is dead!" he says, dropping his hammer and dancing around the wall, his feet like suction cups keeping him in place.

Mussolini doesn't see the blow coming, a low kick to the left knee that dislodges him and sends him spiraling down the pit.

The Being holds on, its fingers grabbing some poor bastard's nose. It had transported up, leaving only a facsimile of itself, that the Italian dictator's doppelganger struck down.

77

"I need to save my energy, one more teleportation and I'll not be able to fight," says the Being, forever climbing upwards.

Near the top, it can see a blue light, like a force field separating the realm and its existence.

It was the toilet water.

The Being gets close to the water, then jumps in it, swimming upwards until the bowl is in sight.

Strange forces act upon the Being upon its arrival at the bowl's event horizon. It feels its size expanding, and with a final thrust, it's launched upwards and out, into the woman's bathroom.

Except that it isn't a bathroom anymore.

The mall has collapsed and rearranged itself around the toilet. It is now just a never ending field of death and destruction, a desert of insanity, filled with wild beasts. Giant postmen, dogs in hats, winged anacondas, ramen soldiers with chicken nugget swords and shields, the green men, now the size of trolls.

In the center of it all, several feet distant from the toilet, the Janitor sits in a throne, while the Monster, in its zoot suit and fedora, laments at his feet.

"Why did Patty leave, Janitor? I was such a good Monster to her."

"There, there. You be a good Monster and leave all that behind. You have a balloon freak to kill and consume."

The Monster's eye light up with the mention of the Being.

"Yes, yes! That motherfucker will pay! Nobody steals my petunias *and* my cat and gets away with it. My children of insanity, defiler of dreams, kill that balloon!" he says, screaming and running towards the Being. He takes of his clothes and transforms into a giant squid with elephant legs, purple and black.

"Good," says the Being as it positions itself for battle. "This is written."

It runs and clashes with a nearby dog. Light whips emerge from its hands, and slice through the dog like butter, the divided halves disentegrating after death.

What follows is a battle of epic proportions. The Being is more than the sum of its parts, it has transcended into something else. It fights the beasts, slicing and stomping, punching and piercing, covering itself in the blood of the wild animals and noodle sauce.

Anacondas try to coil around its hands, but it is faster, and is able to rip them in half before they can finish wrapping around the limb.

Nugget shields are no match for light whips and the Being's mighty punches, its hands like cinder blocks, its appetite so voracious, it devours the noodles, slurping and making great noise, enough to bother a thousand restaurants.

Green men, despite their newly massive size, are no match for the Being's skilled blows. Green men blood washes the floor, as they die screaming.

The Monster and the Being finally engage in battle.

Whips against tentacles, they clash ferociously. The Being is successful in cutting several of the Monster's tentacles down, but for each one it cuts, one and a half sprout in its place, the half being something resembling a baby's chubby arm, without the hand.

"You will die, die, die, die, die, die, die," chants the Monster.

"My victory is written," says the Being.

It pierces the squid's head with a whip, a blow so quick and precise, no tentacle can deflect.

"This can't be," says the Monster.

"Help meeeeee," he screams, pointing towards the

Janitor, who watches everything from his throne.

"That's enough!" screams the Janitor. "I've had it with your interference, balloon. It's time to finish this."

"My thoughts exactly," says the Being, its whip making a jerking motion, cutting the Monster in half.

"I'll feed on it, and I'll become more powerful than you can even imagine! HAHAHAHAHA!" the Janitor says, bursting into millions of bubbles, that flow towards the dead body of the Monster. They wrap around it, and begin to feed on it, so fast it only takes seconds for the squid body to be completely consumed.

A disenbodied voice.

"You shouldn't have fucked with me, Boy Benjamin!"

The voice chants, words that weren's pronounced since the beginning of time itself.

Everything begins to rumble. The last structures collapse, the ground opens up and swallows several wild beasts, dead or alive. They scream inhuman sounds as they are sucked into the void between worlds.

The fallen god's flesh begins to converge towards the bubbles. It swirls and builds up, taking shape.

The Being can see the Janitor reassembled right before the remains collapse around him, as a giant takes shape, the shape of the Janitor himself.

"I AM YOUR GOD, BENJAMIN. FEAR ME," it says, a voice booming so loud, several beasts die just by hearing it.

"Let's go," says the Being, running towards it.

The Uber Janitor is so massive, the Being is only as tall as its ankles.

The Being charges, and swings the whips around, creating deep cuts on the giant's feet.

"HA. HA. HA. Your puny light weapons have no effect on me."

The giant Janitor sweeps down and tries to scoop the Being up, but it's too slow, and the Being is extremely agile. It jumps and parkours around the giant's attempts.

"You are no match for ME," the last word ponctuated by another failed scoop.

The Being shows no sign of fatigue.

"This realm will die," says the giant.

He produces giant orbs, that appear scattered around the land. Each orb is completely black, but filling up with a white light from the bottom up.

"We're out of the critical line, Benjamin. The Nexus is close, and those are zeroes. Once they're fully grown, there will be nothing left to fight for."

"You die, they die. That's all I need to worry about," says the Being.

The giant smirks.

"It will be my pleasure watching you try, freak!" it says, and brings both fists down, hard.

The Being, having anticipated that, rolls in between the fists and delivers the blow.

Two massive whips lashed at each of the giant's eyes. They both pop, and expel a fetid grey ooze.

"AHHHHHHHHHHH!" the giant screams. In a desperate final act, it closes both hands fast, smashing the Being in between them.

"I'll die, but I'm TAKING YOU WITH ME!" the giant says, his voice now a mere shadow of what it was.

"Vengeance is ours!" a voice says.

"Wait, what? Nooooooo...," screams the giant, as the grey ooze takes the shape of the souls in the toilet realm. They all converge on the giant's face, and begin to scratch and bite and pound on it.

The lost souls take their revenge on the giant Janitor. All

frustration and pain they had in life is taken out in the giant false god.

With its last breath, the orbs, now almost fully grown, break down, and explode into millions of pieces of glass, each one burrowing in the ground, becoming a seed. New functions will be born from them, complex functions that will define new realities.

The grey people turn to the Being.

Its body was smashed from the neck down. Its head, the smilling yellow balloon, reverted back to being immobile, just a drawing in latex.

"You're one of us," says one of the grey ooze people. Karen.

"You're free, Benjamin, finally free," she says. The ooze versions of the noseless girl and Mr. Vinogradov put a hand on each one of her shoulders.

"I love you," she says, as she disentangles the ballon's string from the Boy's body.

The giant died holding the Being's body in place, but the grey people, after Karen gently grabs Benjamin, destroy the hands, freeing the Boy's body, that falls gently on the floor.

"Go now, Benjamin. Existence is yours to do as you please. The function is safe and the hypothesis is proved: All of the non-trivial zeroes really do lie on the critical line."

Benjamin says nothing.

Karen flicks Benjamin up, and a gush of wind picks him up. Down below, the beasts feed on the Boy's carcass, his own Existence beginning somewhere else.

Benjamin flies upwards, passing through the mall's ceiling, through the clouds, by the gods playing soccer on the moon and exchanging hot date stories. He passes by himself from another time, sees himself eating noodles and petting Fred with a stringy hand, with Leonhard the Funny

Ant eating scraps from the floor.

He flies towards a new version of the mall, very much like the old version, compeltely restored. But in this version, nobody wants nothing from him, he just exists.

Wires'R'Us. He flies by the stores window, and sees what the green men saw that first night.

It was in fact beautiful. Benjamin now understands why the green men would be drawn to it. It was something that had so much power, it could create Existences on its own.

Benjamin passes through the glass, an ethereal Being made from bits and pieces of reality. He stares at the object, in awe of its presence. And finally, he enters it.

***

"You're awfully quiet, dear, what's on your mind?"

Benjamin looks out the bookstore's window, careful not to move not even an inch, as the bookseller talks to him. His hat is balancing dangerously on his head, and the last thing he wants is to draw her attention more than necessary.

"Please, Benji, talk to me."

He wasn't always called Benjamin. In fact, he wasn't called anything. He simply existed.

Benjamin is a cardboard box. His flaps are a bit torn from prolonged usage. His purpose is to carry things, from the mundane to the irreplaceable. And for him, this is the best life he could ever dream of.

Existence is perfect just the way it is.

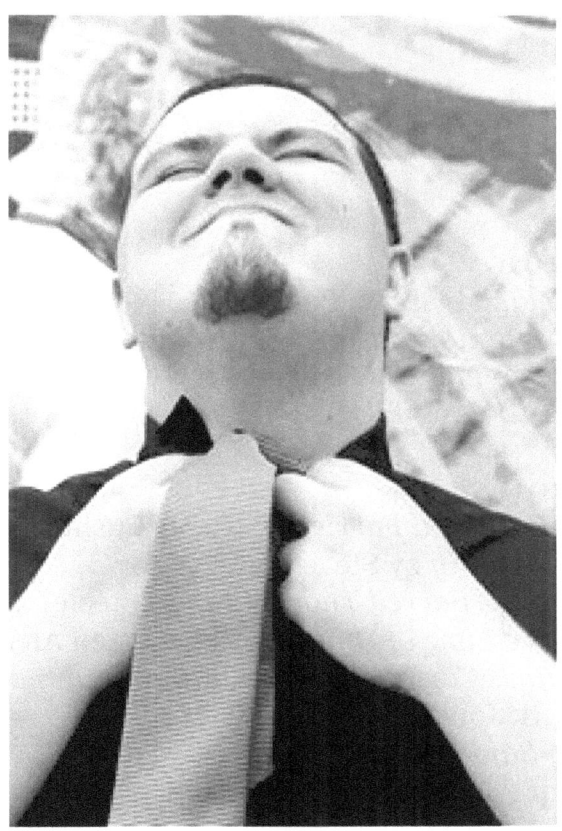

Pedro Proença writes, plays bass and Magic: The Gathering and has a boring day job. You can find him on Facebook and Twitter. He lives in Rio de Janeiro with his family.

The New Bizarro Author Series

2009-2010
Carnageland by D.W. Barbee
Naked Metamorphosis by Eric Mays
Sex Dungeon for Sale by Patrick Wensink
Rotten Little Animals by Kevin Shamel

2010-2011
How to Eat Fried Furries by Nicole Cushing
Muscle Memory by Steve Lowe
Felix and the Sacred Thor by James Steele
Love in the Time of Dinosaurs by Kirsten Alene
Uncle Sam's Carnival of Copulating Inanimals
    by Kirk Jones
The Egg Said Nothing by Caris O'Malley
Bucket of Face by Eric Hendrixson

2011-2012
A Hollow Cube is a Lonely Space by S.D. Foster
Lepers and Mannequins by Eric Beeny
Party Wolves in My Skull by Michael Allen Rose
Seven Seagulls for a Single Nipple
    by Troy Chambers
Gigantic Death Worm by Vince Kramer
The Placenta of Love by Spike Marlowe
Trashland A Go-Go by Constance Ann Fitzgerald
The Crud Masters by Justin Grimbol

2012-2013
Gutmouth by Gabino Iglesias
Janitor of Planet Anilingus
  by Andrew Wayne Adams
House Hunter S.T. Cartledge
Avoiding Mortimer by J.W. Wargo
Her Fingers by Tamara Romero
Kitten by G. Arthur Brown

2013-2014
The Mondo Vixen Massacre by Jamie Grefe
The Cheat Code for God Mode by Andy De Fonseca
Babes in Gangland by Bix Skahill
8-bit Apocalypse by Amanda Billings
Grambo by Dustin Reade
There's No Happy Ending by Tiffany Scandal
The Church of TV as God by Daniel Vlasaty

2014-2015
SuperGhost by Scott Cole
Pax Titanus by Tom Lucas
Deep Blue by Brian Auspice

2015-2016
King Space Void by Anthony Trevino
Rainbows Suck by Madeleine Swann
Arachnophile by Betty Rocksteady
Benjamin by Pedro Proenca
Rock 'n' Roll Head Case by Lee Widener
Slasher Camp for Nerd Dorks by Christoph Paul
Elephant Vice by Chris Meekings
Pixiegate Madoka by Michael Sean Le Sueur
Towers by Karl Fischer